BLOOD AND ROSES

JACK TOWNSON

D1253632

Jack
Townson

For my amazing boys
For the woman who made this all possible,
And for the Fangfam, without all of whom I would truly
be lost.

FOREWORD

This anthology is more than just words written on paper, it is a love letter to not only the character I've created, but to the found family I've made. To the community of the FangFam, to the supporters that have watched my journey over the years, to the woman I love who has inspired me to finally put my passion out there for all to see, but also to myself and to my boys whom I love with all of my soul. I hope this makes them proud.
- Jack Townson

THE VAMPIRE'S WIFE

She sits with pursed ruby lips and stares
out the window

The rain spraying like fresh sea foam on
autumn mornings when the boats are
docked

Her daydreams of the darkness defying
the tyrannous rays that pierce the
overcast

Fangs sink into the foundries of even her
earliest recollection

Raven hair wrapped about icy features,
gothic garb of old forgotten days

Talons clutching red strands to their

*breast- begging "drink, and know
eternity"*

*The longing that never comes, yet she
waits- creates- never lets it abate*

*Until one day, that is, when a voice comes
to call*

*A dark angular creature, shrouded in
gloom and fall
With jagged digits to rake up her exposed
backbone
"Finally, my dear, I knew it was you all
along"*

*And with outstretched limb to pull her to
She finds salvation, through and through*

-For Shayne Leighton-Townson, the
woman who saved me from my
darkness

THE SEER

Dust pours from pooled orbs
Blackened with the descent of madness
There is nothing but the call
"Father, mother!"
A worm that slithers and wiggles
Finding purchase within minds foundry
Wisdom comes at such a price
An oracle of blindness

A FLAME OF MY MAKING

Flames
They lick as lovers do
Ever consuming, never to release
A warmth I yearned for- yet now regret
She clings to me, this fire
Nothing compares to the sweet smell
Of burning flesh

THE CROSS

Petals caressed with care
My fingers, do touch and entice
With promise of love and laughter
Of new life and awakening
Of kindred unity and understanding
Yet, I release the delicate thing
And allow it to shatter upon my feet
Left in the cold, I taught it pain
And the meaning of resentment

DEAR CHLOE

Somewhere beyond waking, she calls
Beckons me home with open arms
The broken place we both grew frail
Yet, stronger side by side
A faint smile fixed in place
Our fingers touch as she pulls
And as she does they crack and wane
As we wither into dust
... I have to stay away...

CARVER

Gnarled digits snap and bend
Clutched together in equal under-
    standing
Of power, of order, of control
The scepter lays upon his lap
The crown upon his head
All ears open to his croak
All eyes watching for his next move
Royalty
Or is it a lie...
Is he a serpent in disguise

HOOK SYNDROME

"Tik tok", says the croc
The beast it hungers still
"Im waiting in your belly, dear
When is our next kill?"
I thrash and cry, moan and scream
Yet my protests fall to deafness
I need to run back home my love
I hope they left me breakfast...

AIDEN PIERCE

Screaming
This twisted pain that bubbles and boils
Burning heat of unbridled fury
The remembrance of agony lost and
    found
I cry for help, yet on deaf ears they fall
I am nothing but a babe abandoned
And as the rain falls on my broken corpse
I remember each blood tear shed
From the very utterance of his name

THE TOREADOR

With a wiggle of my finger the
   world bows
With a wave of my hand they gasp in awe
With a smile they giggle bashfully
And when I weep they rush to coddle
All the while
With a fang toothed smile
I feast from their adoration
I blush and bloom and flourish
While the poor fools whither at my touch
A kiss is never so simple

PORCELAIN

I wore what you asked
Strapped in chains of purity
A porcelain smile, kept and contained
Your puppet, your lie
Your ivory Hyde
Kept buried beneath silk and sanity
We spun secrets
Wrote symphonies
Laughed blood soaked giggles
Yet, you couldn't truly tame me

THE CROWN

The Crown
Seated neatly
Shining with order and purpose
It barks commands and demands
    obedience
None may question
None may falter
To rise is to be Damned
Tossed aside and left broken and
    discarded
To fall is freedom
To dance, to dive
To plummet ever so dangerously
To meet with stone far beneath
Freedom is pain
Obedience is complacency
To be the sheep in the herd
Or to be a wolf, singular and fierce
The crown

It demands obedience
Perhaps it is as they say
It is better rule in hell than to serve in
*   heaven*
To dance with the devil, free

MAKER

Sweet urchin
Sleep tight within my embrace
Nothing here shall you fear
For I am close
Hush sweet child
Close your eyes
Hear nothing but sweet lullabies
Know no fear or the pain of truth
Or the world beyond my eyes
Sink deep in my heart and know
My love, my soul, they are yours
All I am I give to you
All I was I leave to you
All I have you may claim
For you are all I wish for
Your love is everything
Your joy means worlds
And you, as well, are mine

A KISS

Your love so deep and dark
Pools of pain that touch my heart
Through the pain I see your soul
And I am lost forever more

Your lips so sinisterly sweet
That Taste good enough to eat
Euphoric cries with no measure
And I am bound to your kiss forever

You are agony, of the sweetest kind
That voice it ravages my mind
Your touch it stains down to my bone
I'll keep you now, you are my home

RAVENMADE

Raven mane of feather's oil
Twisted mangled heart of coils
Lips so sinister they burn
An image in your mind
Voice of lavender and silk
That speak of the deepest ilk
Which cry of deep woods and old huts
Where the crones mix and give their
    blessings
Skin of overcast, a memory of sunshine
    gone
Her beauty screams of old ways
Of dark days
An all consuming enticing blaze
Bewitching
Unflinching
Unwavering curses
I am hers

LYCANTHROPE

Tonight I ran
Unshackled
Unbound
The wind ripping through each strand
I had forgotten
A king of beasts unbridled runs free
A memory to slay mortal fears
A wolf
There is no lycanthrope my equal
I had forgotten the majesty
Of fur through autumn leaves
Each claw shredding bark upon tree
Each tuft of raven dancing
As I weep through howls
At the beauty
Of unrestrained
Freedom

SHADOW

The scent of shadow
It returns to my nostrils
The stench of putridity I had forgotten
As the blood calls me home I remember
A memory of bitterness and disdain
Her face. My talons. Her throat.
I am a babe again crying in the moonlight
And she, the flesh I hold to my bosom

Begging

"Feed... feed."

A WORLD AWAY

In time and space I find you
Floating, untouched, imperfect
A symbol of chaos and tranquility
In this place we see one another
And I am forever changed

In this place you found me
Shattered, discarded, perfection
A symbol of bliss and mystery
In this place we are blind
To the world and what pain it brings

Here we are equal
Here we are trapped
A place between expectations
Where dreams go to die

And here is where I keep you.

Here is where you know me.
Beyond is meaningless,
This is all that matters.

BEAUTIFUL AGONY

In glass intwined
She sits
Aching beautiful agony
Sweet sinister lips
My mirrored soul
She sits
Love, sweet love
Burning twisted pleasure
Tainted by my touch
I call her mine, forever
She sits
Waiting
Writhing
The reflection of a goddess

I saved them for her
Pages burned and tattered
Mended with mangled claw
Scribbled phantom words of wolf

Written lions roar

She ignites me, this twisted thing
Sets my love aflame
Rakes my soul across the coals
Then makes me whole again

Through the flames she takes firm grasp
My heart pulsing in her palm
A decision she could make, any time
To smother or to calm?

Would she,
she could and even that would be enough
No
The twisted thing, scorched and changed
She holds the lump softly still
Cares for it, molds it
Until...

What once was broken stands renewed

THE TASTE OF BONE

With a tug of my hand you pulled me
    to you
Such soft digits wrapped in mine
And with the tug I fell against
Your soft warm skin with scent divine

And I kissed your lips
Though, in horror
I found none there
Just brittle bone
Stripped and bare

Yet I still tasted what you wished
Bitterness

And loved you even still...

THE ROSE AND THE THORN

Ruby red strands with boundless ire
Licked with sun kissed blessed fire
A voice of sirens that beckons me home
Across the thorns, tear through to bone
My heart delights sadistic charm
Her name a curse with woven arm
She calls to me, this siren song
Pulls me though the abysmal throng
Caresses my petals and keeps them bright
Carries my bouquet with her through the
    night
Holds me to her, I almost let go
This heart is hers, she'll always know
And with skilled fingers, she prunes the
    edges
Removes said blades from guarded hedges
Allowing passage betwixt once more
To the lump still bruised and sore
And with calm hand she cradles it still

Keeps it safe and fed with thrill
Until a beat can be once heard
Then twice it's former, and then a third
Until a steady rhythmic thump
Awakens my heart a final jump
The thorns which kept others at bay
Quickly trimmed and brushed away
To allow the one who holds it true
My darling, please see this is you....
Of all the loves and lives I've known
No other has ever felt like home...

AUTUMN'S FLAME

Through the trees I see them fall
Like paper planes and porcelain dolls
The leaves they change each passing day
Come to take my dread away
And in the mist of fogged night
The creatures come to my delight
To drag the corpses from their homes
And wrestle free their sleeping bones
For in the darkness a pale moon creeps
A crooked smile with broken teeth
It gnashes as it glares through beams
A terror no one could have seen
And in the darkness of my mind
I see the truth as it unwinds
Like a clock's last hand to fall
The flame of autumn comes to call
It's fire billows a roaring groan
And I remember... I am home

BLOOD AND ROSES

Clawed hands entwine
Fingers locked gracefully
Piercing cries of dark divine
Our words entangled permanently
Across vast oceans I would ride
To bring her home, purposefully
To claim the love which I call mine
Here in my grasp, eternally

And she purrs under my clutches,
She writhes, squirms, and begs
Calls this monster her master
And gushes to every digits twitch

To scream, to bleed for her
Without a second thought

THE SILVER TAIL OF MIDNIGHT

This looks like the end of the story; but it
   isn't.

Pages scattered. Forgotten. Black words
   bleed over and into the carpet.

Shallow breathing, laying in this space
   where ink sinks away like blood from
   flesh stories.

Night consumes the space. Swallows me
   whole. For a moment, it is all empty.

But there—is it a shadow? Is it a trick?

Or does the angel not arrive on the jagged
   back of dawn?

Maybe, instead, he rides in on the silver
    tail of midnight.

When things seem bleakest, he appears
    with one wing. It's broken. His
    feathers are a mess.

Does dark surround, or do stars appear?

I reach. I strain to see.

He is really there.

Not heralded by golden light— instead,
    shadow signals his presence;

And calls me home.

- Shayne Leighton

TOXIC

Her fingers intwine and grasp
Keeping mine close, never to release
Her cries of passion rake the sky
We are one in our furious lust

JACK

Bring me your young and your starving
   your weary and fame obsessed.

Come to me and I'll show you a world
   you could not imagine.

You wish to be someone, don't you?

You wish to dance in starlight and
   twinkle upon the stage.

I can do this for you, and more.

Together, we can make you burn brighter
   than any sunlight,

and I will yearn for you just as much.

PAIN

Pain is both joy and misery
As the trickle of blood can be erotic or
    deadly
It sends the nervous system spiraling
Yet, deep within it is one we yearn for
To cry and bleed and scream
Yet with those words do I speak of horror
Or of lust
We are primitive creatures
Clawing for a thirst we do not understand
To be buried deep within
Writhing on a cold floor
As waves of sensation take us
Is it murder if both parties delighted in it

WALKING DISGRACE

Desolate, alone, defeated.

Broken hearted love soaked bleeding.

Nothing but the darkest hues,
of a demon in my view.

Tormentor, aflame for all to see,
wrapped in chains of cacophony.

A monster left in the dust of your wake,
my soul is forever discarded.

I am blind for I see,
I am dead but ever living,
I am remorse with no guilt.
I am nothing to no one, everything to all.
I am senseless, void.

Eternally your walking disgrace.

Monsters get no sympathy.

Once upon a time I had no voice
Now I have one Yet no one listens
My cries quelled With deafening silence
My blood torn Left and unfiltered
No sympathy For a monster
Veins of rust Carry ash that is mean-
     ingless
Forgotten lineage of a broken path
Clawed hands rake the sky
Yet all they catch is nothing but air
Pain, agony unrelenting
Yet at least I feel

I TRIED

Today is a day I never saw coming
A realization that so much I do means
     nothing
That every word I write
Is just a desperate cry
For attention, love, or something
I'm a loser and I know it, no questions
     needed
Answers that I spit out never heeded
I'll just sit back and laugh as this world
     burns around me

What's the use when what you do goes
     unseen
Paliachi was a joker, laughed through
     tears blue
And I'll never be right, complete because
     of you

Of the darkness that you hid beneath a
    veil so true

That even your mother had to get you to
    put it to

I'm so tired of writing these fucking songs
Every poem dashed in blood just like
    funeral psalms

And on the chance that you saw them,
    your own words numb

Not a cry for help or even impressed upon
Just neglect and defect and move the
    fuck on
You're a big boy now, a man, come on
You can take it, every hit every sorrow
You're a big fucking boy suck it up for
    tomorrow

I guess I just don't get it anymore,

I'm not perfect. Im not good, but I strive
    to be more.

For family, for my boys, for my wife
    even too.
For friends who are alcoholics and pieces
    of shit through and through.

It doesn't matter the wrapping, just the

pain held within,

And we're all guilty of forgetting who's
human.
I'm not. Am I? I don't fucking know.

I was the boy who survived, then thrown
out the door

Ain't I special, son of a whore bitch and
Jack the Ripper

A murderers boy, sent up the river
Out of resentment and no pity,
Get this fucking demon out of me!
Send it away and don't let come back
Oh, on a second thought, fuck that
Here's the painting I made for this poor
little urchin

Some breadcrumbs to leave for this boy to
hone in

Leave on the back, my names of the lion
And watch how thirty fuckin years fly
by him
Begging for peace of mind and truth
Like fates mocking "answers right in front
of you"

THE CHASE

In darkness we met
Predator and Prey
Our chase at an end
Together we play
An entanglement of limbs
A bloody bouquet
Your lips on my skin
I can't stay away
And each night that I fight
I fall further astray
So it's time to give in
I'll keep you all day

THE WOLF AND THE LION

Black fur
Storm cloud ash
Tapestry of battle and pain
The wolf howls
Alone
Solitary
Needing of no one, it stalks the darkness
A glint of blue betrays its heart
Eyes of sea soft and fair tides
Yet the heart within at constant unrest

Wild unkempt mane
Dark and furrowed brow
A body built for the hunt
Eyes of pain staring at a world in mistrust
The lion prowls
A pride of his own yet unfulfilled
Tired of sitting and waiting for the prey to
     be returned

It begins to scour the lands
A visage is beautiful rage
Yet it's heart longs for more

Twisted fang and claw meet
Lightning litters ashen skies
The land covered in bones of past
    conquest
The lords of the gutter clash
And then familiarity finds each eye
A twin snaked pain that slithers and
    screams
Two souls mirrored beneath the fur
Heart beats drumming as one

Talons meet dirt as two titans halt
Slits of gold against orbs of sky
The mane that stood on end falls flat
The arched back calms ever still
Twin souls stare in silence
A moment of recognition

Perhaps neither had to die that day.

Perhaps there could be more.

OF BONES AND BLACK ROSES

Come play in the darkness,

Where the sun dare not show its face.
Where the nightmares are real,
To keep you in this place.

Delve Deep in the shadows where all
    hope is lost,

Where the night creatures roam,

As they watch through the moss.

Creep through the bones of the trees
    wrapped in thorns,

To bask in the leaves where the black
    roses form.

PREDATOR AND PREY

In darkness we met
Predator and Prey
Our chase at an end
Together we play
An entanglement of limbs
A bloody bouquet
Your lips on my skin
I can't stay away
And each night that I fight
I fall further astray
So it's time to give in
I'll keep you all day

IN THE DARK OF THE EVENING

In the dark of the evening
Our bodies collide
Hand over hand,
we no longer hide
Your lips, my skin,
this lust I confide
An entanglement of limbs
why try to fight

BROTHERS IN BLOOD

Two Roses.
Two Brothers.
Two Fates bound together.
Their Destiny Covered in Thorns.
A Sadists Hand,
Would Scour the Land
To Shackle Our boys to his throne.
One Shaped by Oppression,
The Other, Obsession.
Four Wrists Bound in Vines evermore.
The Twin Blooded Souls
Who called him their home
Would war until one found his tome
Six cold and one jaded
Each Twirling Upon a Stage
Set for An Audience of
One

KINDRED

We are Shadows
Silhouettes of self
Ethereally Unseen
From a world undeserving
Hiding who we are
As we prowl through fogged eve
Unchanging, forever fixed
In a state
Of unending
Torment

HEART OF MINE

No sweeter cheeks
That I have seen
None other can compare
Skin of caramel
Like oceans of toffee
And coffee colored hair
Hues of mint swallowed by fair tides
His smile chipped yet holds
On pure chaos does he thrive
In my heart he's home

IMPURE DIVINE

Tattered Wings
A soul discarded
Watching through bloodied globes
A blackened talon upon my chest
I rake the skies in my agony
Cast aside
Tossed to the depths
There is nothing
But the sound
Of torment
And then it comes
From below my cloven feet
A voice which shakes my bones
"Rise, embrace the night"
And I am filled again
My resolve my home

SHAKE THE DEAD

Pry you from your bed
Scream before you're dead
Keep you filled with dread
Drain thoughts from your head

Nightmarish in delight
Almost out of sight
Hiding from the light
Party every night

I shamble through boarded doors
Ripping the sheets from your corpse
Dragging you across the floor
I'm just another horror whore

And in the graveyard we will sing
This mortal shell I do fling
From atop this grassy thing
The bell reverberates a final ring.

BROKEN

Standing over shards of glass
Ripping flesh but it's never deep enough
I press harder
Hoping to feel something for even a
    moment
Even if that feeling is agony
It shows that I'm not what they say I am
Unfeeling, inhuman, a monster
I bleed, therefore I am
I scream, so I must be
These tears may stain my cheeks red
Still, perhaps it could make her see

SKIN OF A KILLER

No sympathy for the devil they said
Just a creature of darkness and pain,
Just a bastard who's crazy they said
Just a killer with no remorse,

And I listened, for so long I listened
I let them undulate within my brain
Like a serpent's tongue to Adam's apple
Like a father holding to his son a bible
Explaining to him how wrong he is for
    how he feels

That the devils inside and it has to deal
Purge this wickedness that I reject
Yet I really wonder what comes next
Am I man or beast
Killer or king

Is there a heart of a lion or the soul of
*   something*
Agony isn't so bad when it's the only
*   feeling you've ever had*

COFFIN DRAGGING

Coffin dragging never felt so right
Feet clinging to the streets at night
Your body screaming in the sheets in
    fright
Gonna party to the morning light

SCREAM FOR THE NIGHT

Growling on all fours

Lock the fucking door

Have you on the floor

Coming back for more

And I purr

And you scream

Between twin legs I am enveloped in the
    passions you spew

AGAINST THE FOREST FLOOR

Deep in the black forest I found it
This thirst I had held off for so long
I had forgotten what it meant to be
An unbridled and untamed monstrosity
Her neck beneath my claws as she does
    twitch
Soft skin pressed firmly against the ditch
Where I keep muffled moans stifled still
My unbeating heart a phantom thumping
    thrill
And as she groans a final plea
I watch said orbs flutter violently
With forked tongue I caress her depths
And dive deep into the fountain of her

FALL FOR YOU

Your lips are October
Warm like apple cider
Hair of fallen leaves
Scattered across a forest floor
Eyes of the summer briefly gone
You are Autumn
And as such
I fall
For you

MY SOUL

In the darkness I belong
Where all I know exists
I rule this place of shadows
For Here I am King
Seated upon a throne
Singular
From the light she reaches for me
My clawed hand in hers
With the pull I am lifted
And we soar upwards
She ascends
And I crash
Back
Down
Where I belong
Alone
Empty
Nothing
With gnarled digits I scrape the dirt

And I remember one truth
In this solitude
I am home
And no one
Can save me
From myself

HER FACE AND THE MOON

Across lunar leaves and forest floors
Slender digits trace the trail

Her melodious tones they rip and roar
My hands at her back my footing fails

From the grove she beckons to me
Her arms outstretched to call me home

A cheshire grin with haunted glee
Towards my demise do I roam

Her weeping willow strands of dread
The wind scatters them as I approach

In the place where Darklings tread
I ignore my mind's reproach

Here

In the darkness

I stay

My phantom jezebel
Goddess of dismay

And as my limbs grow black from rot
My cries are all for naught

ABOUT THE AUTHOR

The Vampire Jack Townson is an actor, live-action role-player, and vampfluencer based on Long Island, New York with a dedicated following on social media of over thirty thousand people. Jack Townson is also a celebrated recording artist and author, but his most important role in his unlife is the one he takes most seriously...father.

For more information about the works of Jack Townson
and upcoming novel series, visit:
www.vampirejacktownson.com

Lightning Source UK Ltd.
Milton Keynes UK
UKHW010637180223
417178UK00005B/419